THE PERFECT FIT

Naomi Jones   James Jones

OXFORD
UNIVERSITY PRESS

This is Triangle.

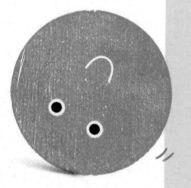

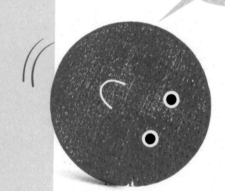

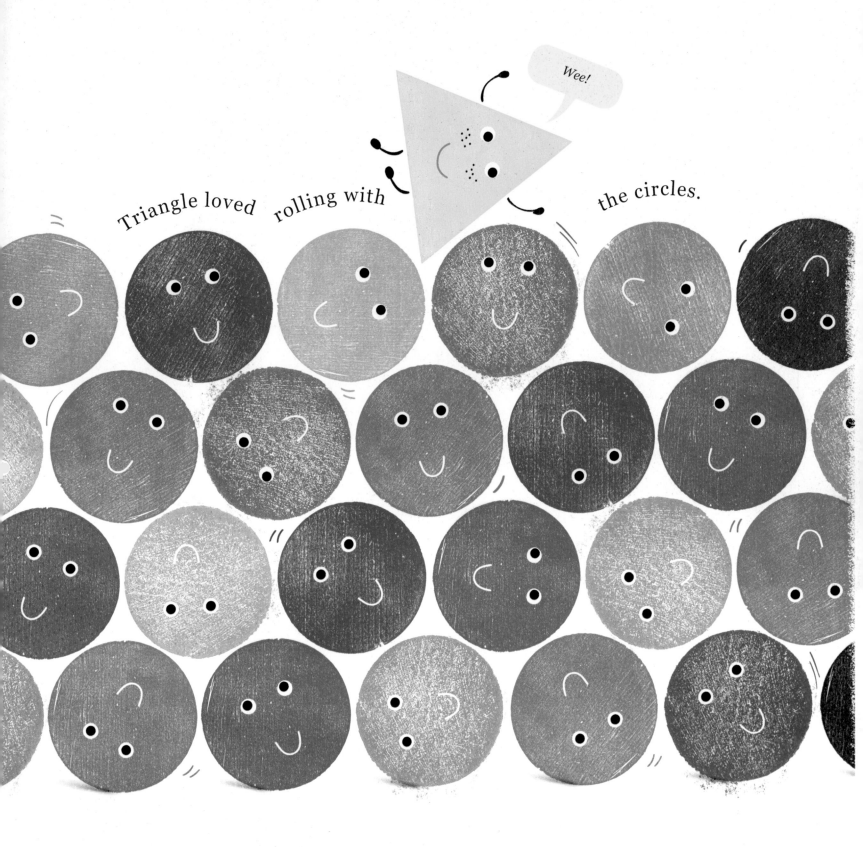

Triangle loved rolling with the circles.

Wee!

But sometimes she
felt a bit *different*.

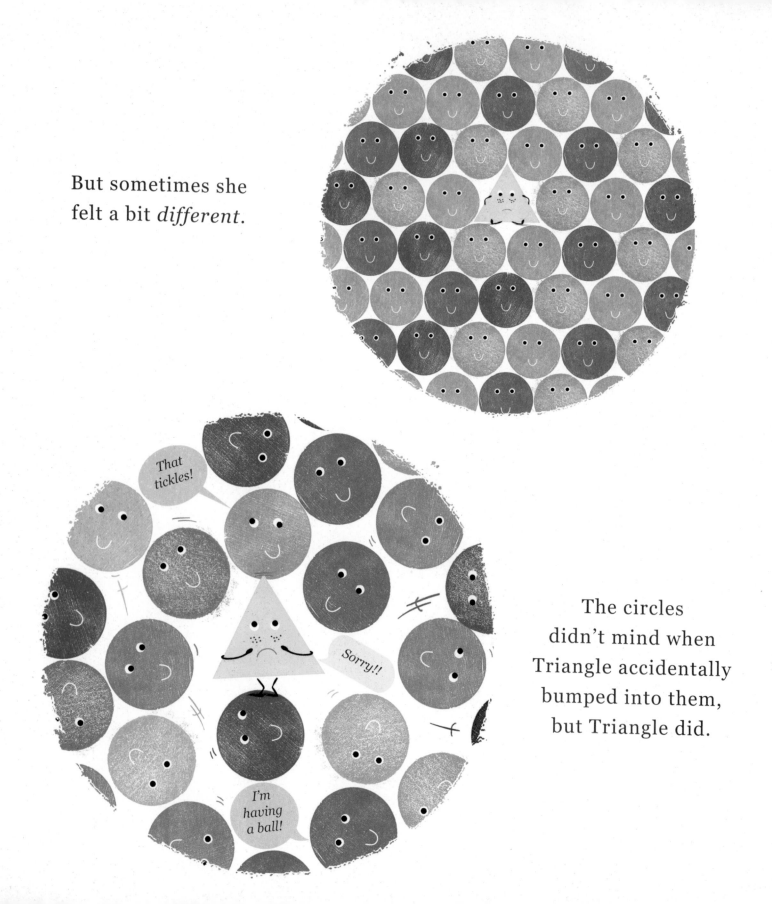

The circles
didn't mind when
Triangle accidentally
bumped into them,
but Triangle did.

She felt
like she
was getting
in their way.

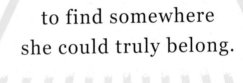

So she decided
to find somewhere
she could truly belong.

Just around the corner,
Triangle discovered
some squares.

'Come and play with us!'
the squares said.

So Triangle did.

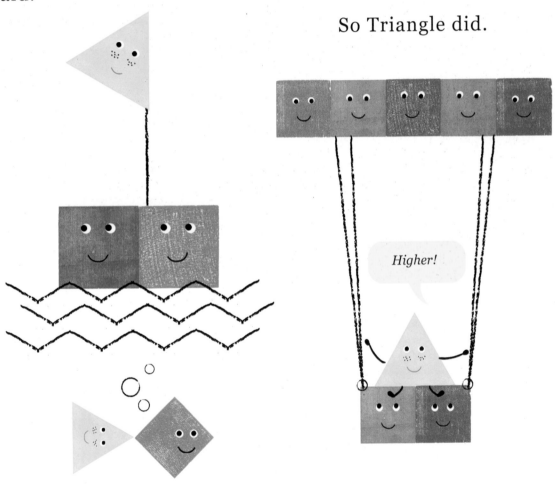

They played all sorts of games and it was brilliant.

'Let's build a tower!'
one of the squares suggested.

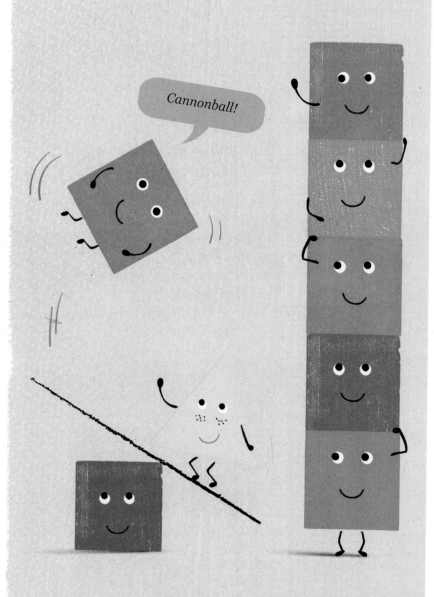

So Triangle
hopped up
to help,

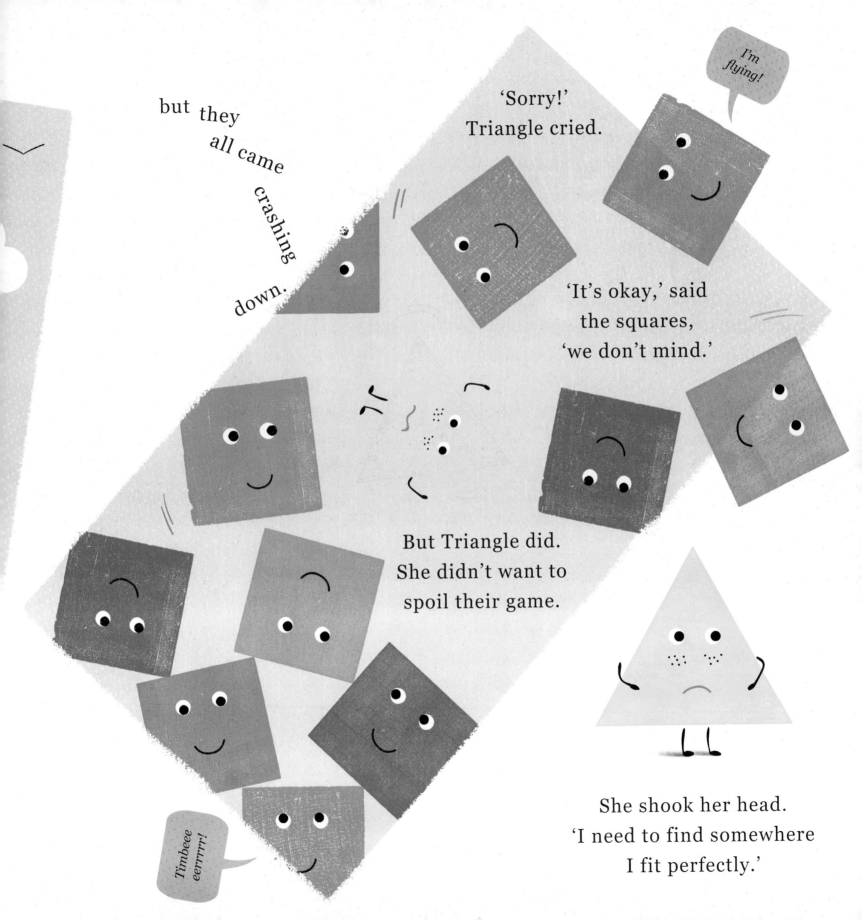

Around the next corner
Triangle found some hexagons.

'Do you want to play?'
they asked. Triangle nodded.

Friend!

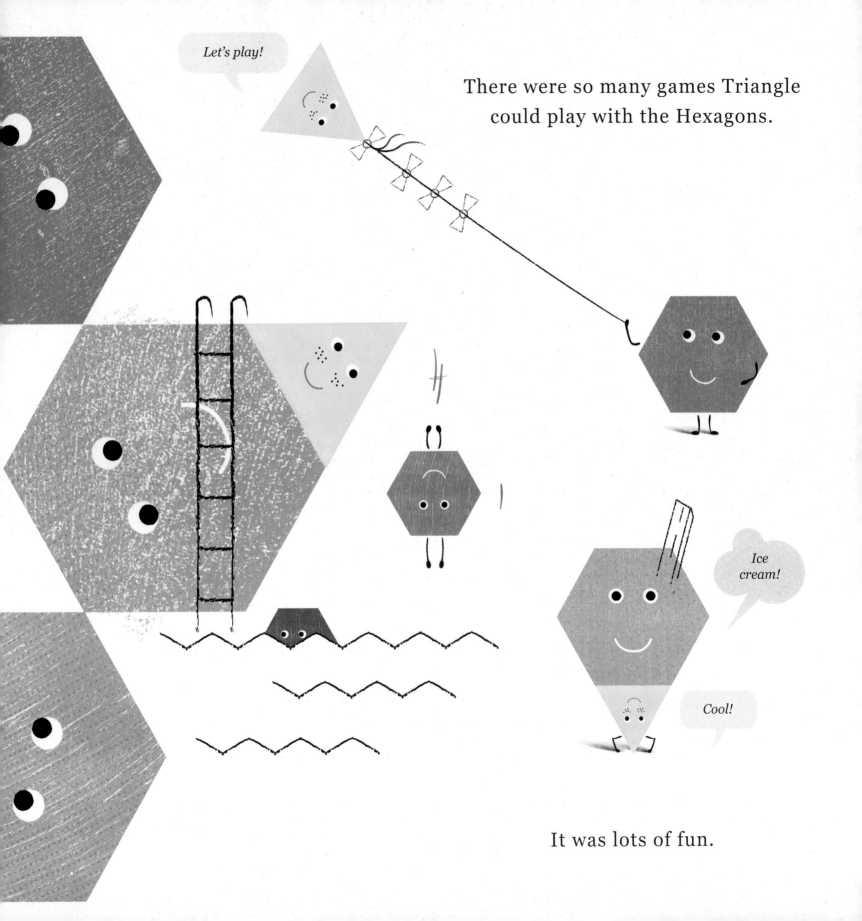

There were so many games Triangle could play with the Hexagons.

It was lots of fun.

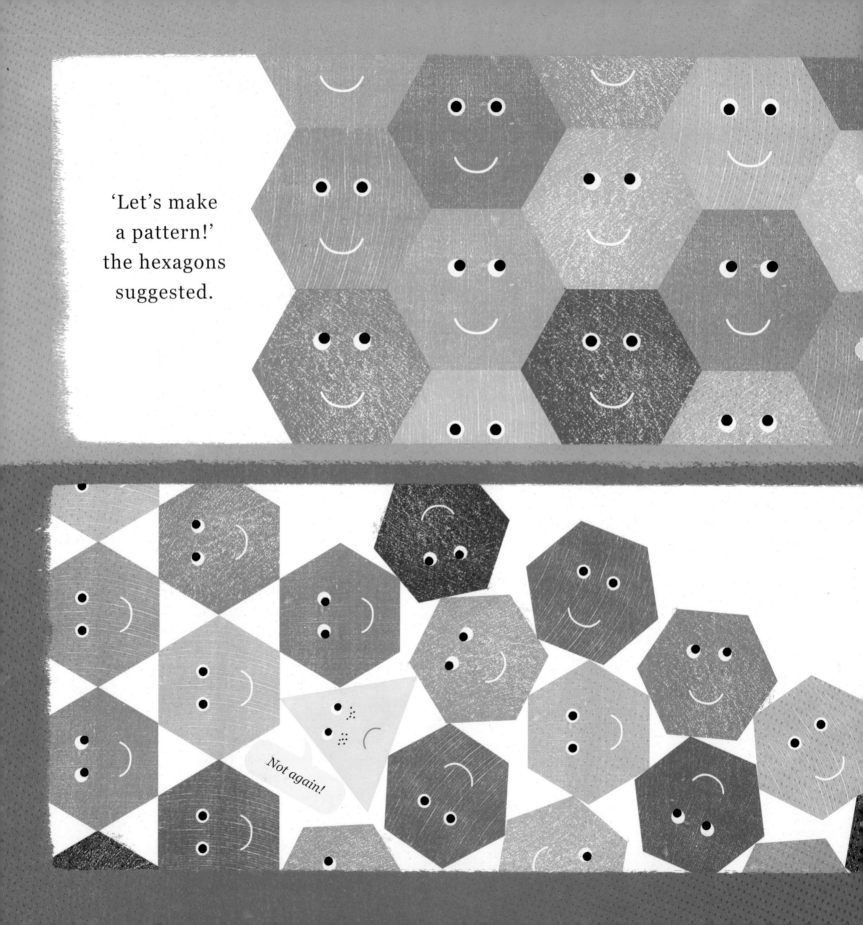

'Let's make a pattern!' the hexagons suggested.

Not again!

Triangle joined in,
but she kept making
the pattern *different*,
not the same.

'We can play
something else?'
the hexagons said.

But Triangle decided to say
goodbye and keep on going.

Triangle searched
and searched . . .

Hello . . .

Anybody
there?

but couldn't find anywhere
she fit perfectly.

Anyone?!

She was starting to
feel very fed up.

'Maybe there aren't any other triangles.'

'Maybe I'm the only one?'

But then she looked up and thought she saw a familiar shape in the sky.

'You're not a triangle are you?' Triangle asked.

'Almost—
but not quite!'
the star said.

Triangle sighed.

'Don't worry,
there are shapes
that look exactly
like you and they're
not that far away . . .'

Finally
she found
them. Triangles
that were exactly the
same as her, in every single
way. She rushed over to join them.

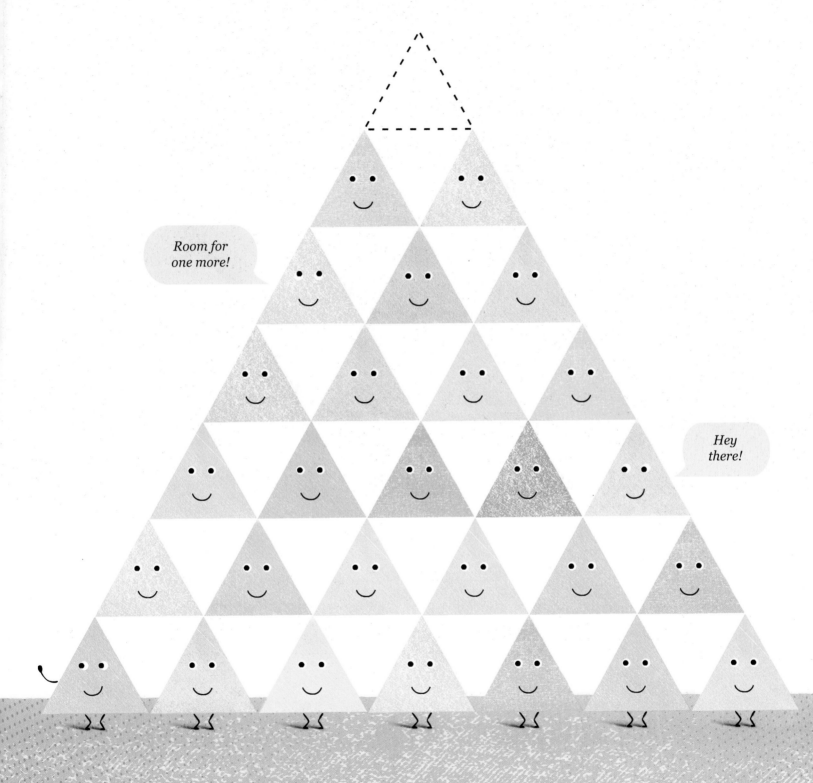

Together they played
lots of triangle games
and it was wonderful.

*Big fan
of this!*

*Merry
Christmas!*

'What shall we do next?'
one of the triangles asked.

Hey star!

Bravo!

'Let's roll!'
Triangle suggested.

But none of
the other triangles
knew how to roll.

As Triangle tried to show them, she thought about all the fun
she'd had with the other shapes and it gave her an idea.

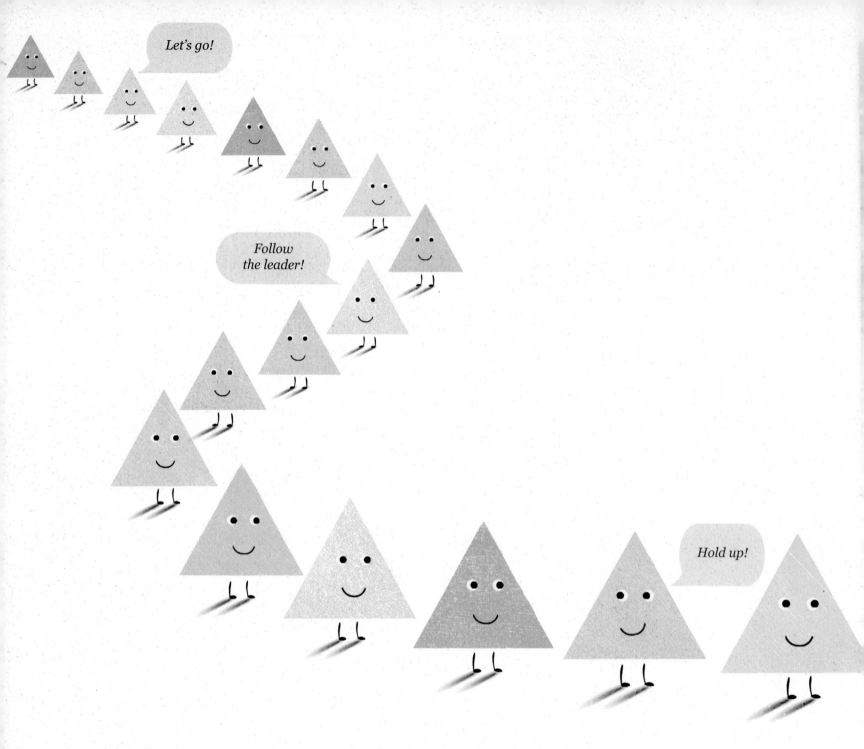

'You found
the others!'
the star
called down.

'I did,' Triangle replied,
'and we had lots of fun.
But I realised there was
something missing . . .

everyone else!'

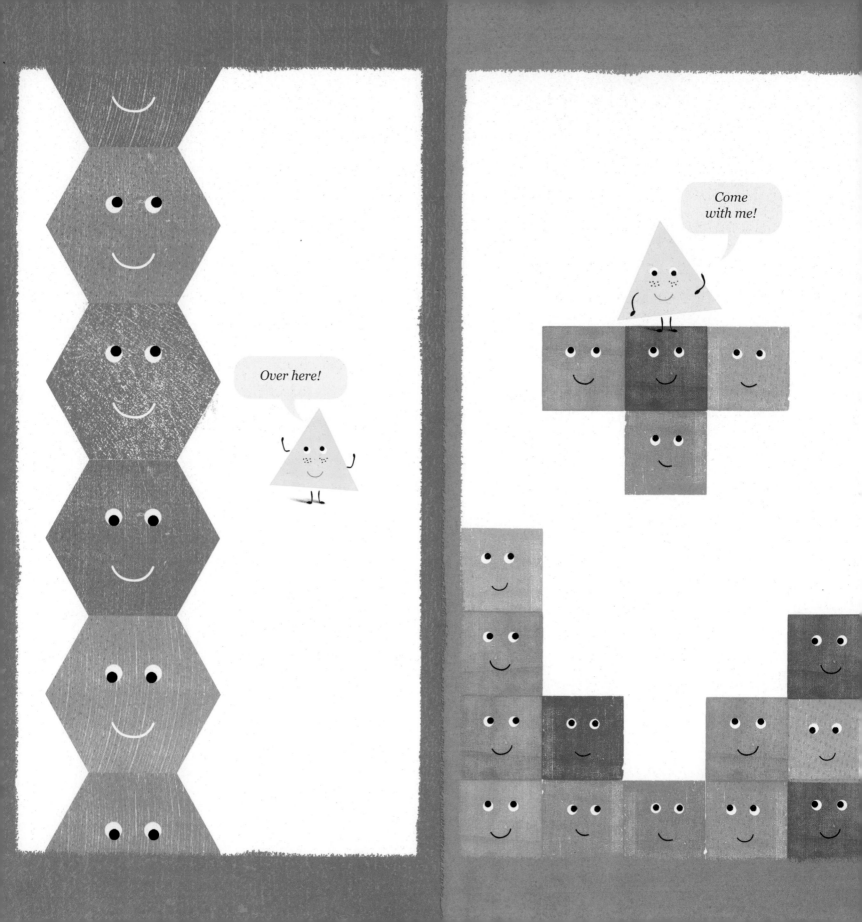

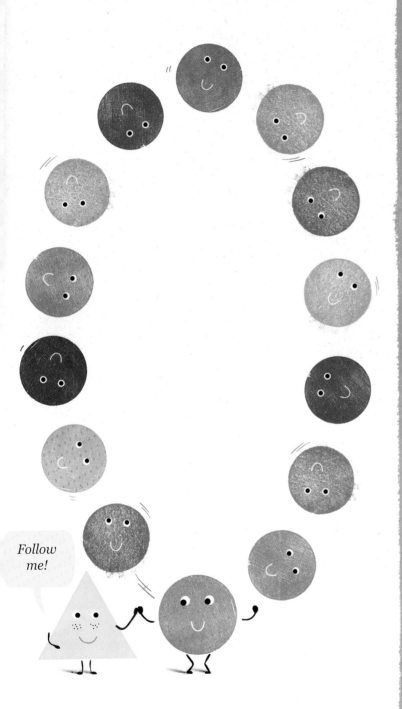

Would you ALL like to
play with me?'

The shapes were very excited.

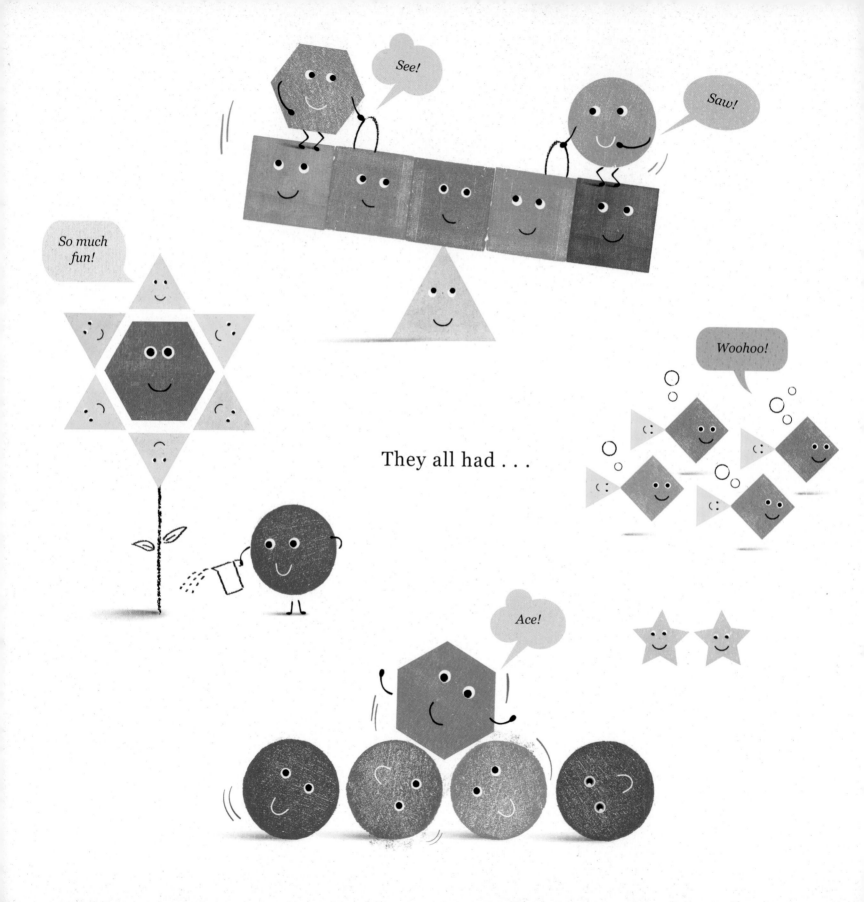

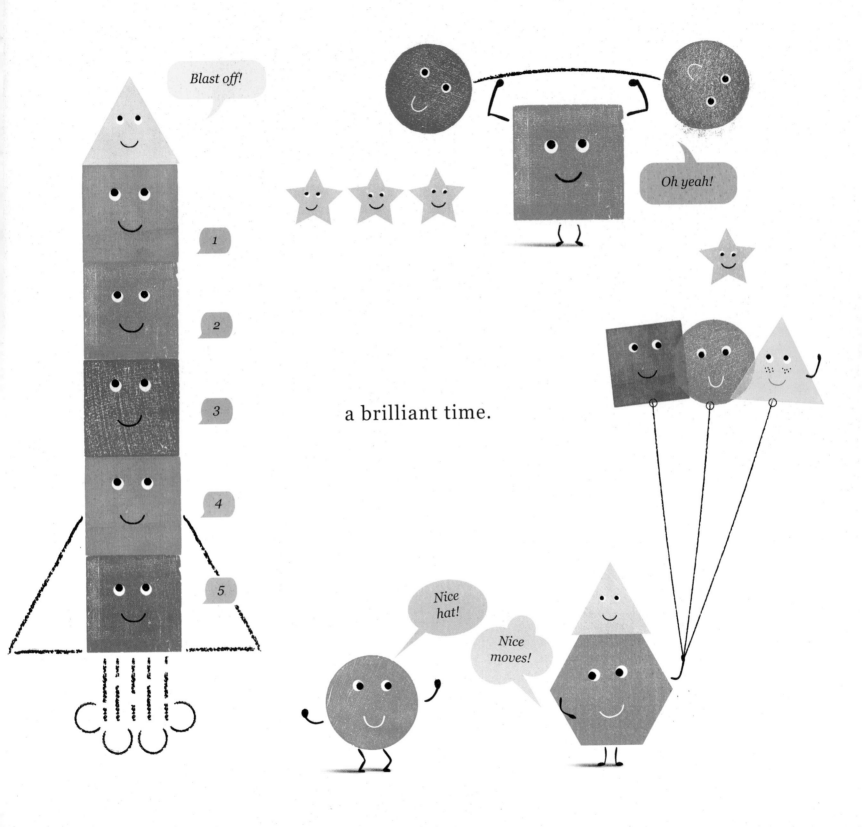

a brilliant time.

And even though

Triangle wasn't exactly

the same as everyone else,

it was
still

a perfect
fit.

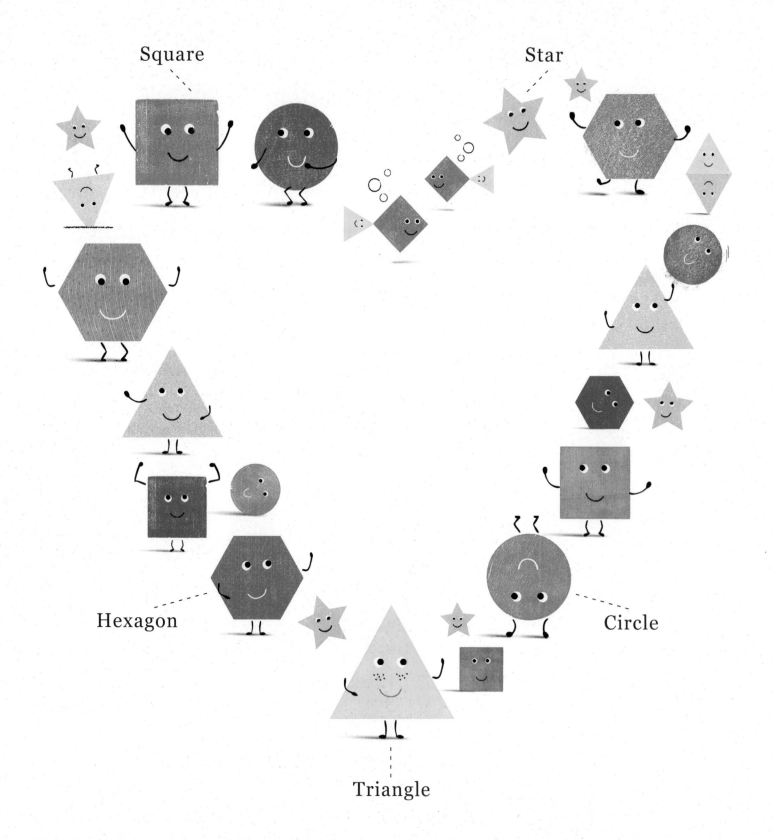

Square

Star

Hexagon

Circle

Triangle